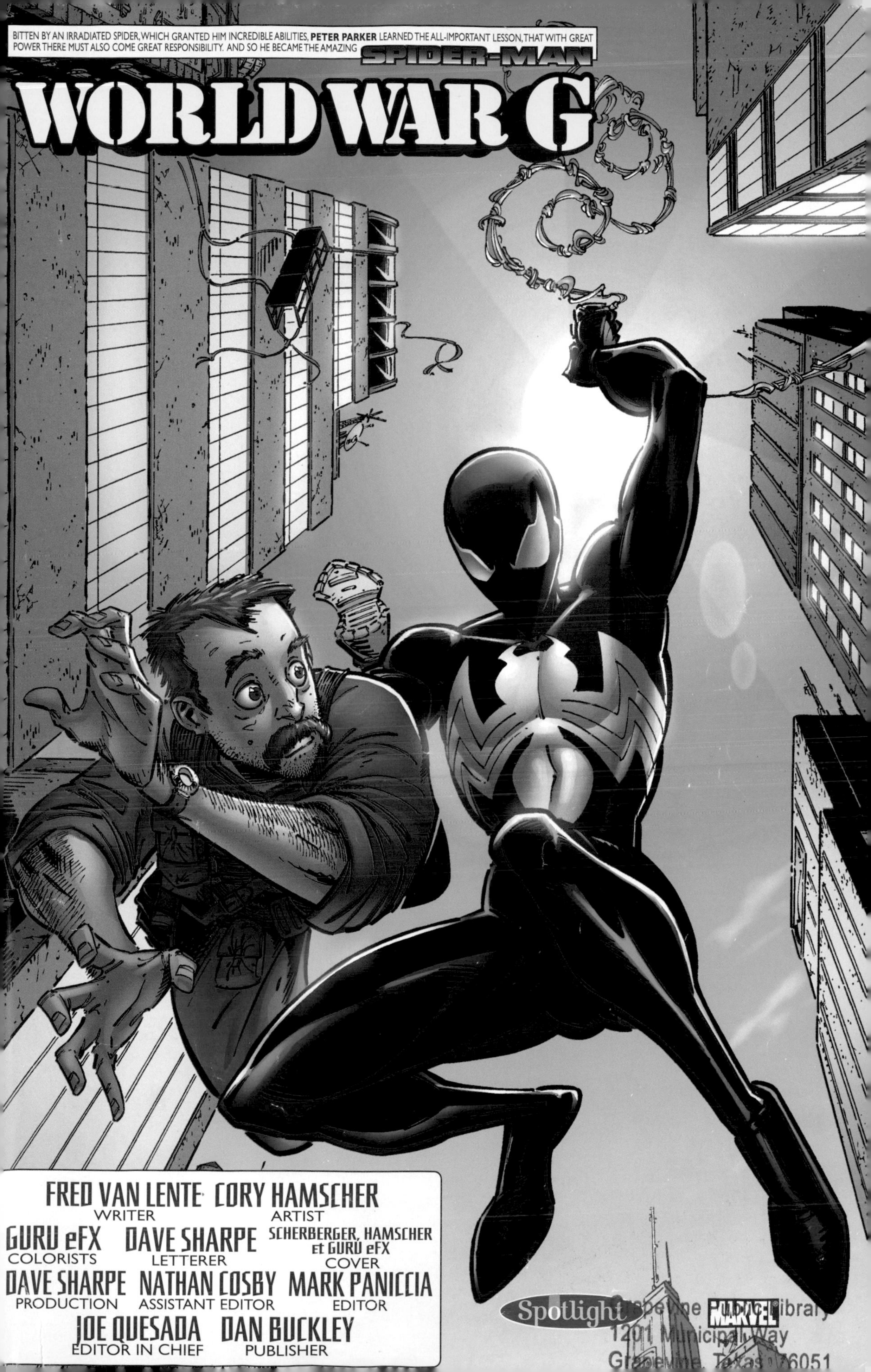
BITTEN BY AN IRRADIATED SPIDER, WHICH GRANTED HIM INCREDIBLE ABILITIES, PETER PARKER LEARNED THE ALL-IMPORTANT LESSON, THAT WITH GREAT POWER THERE MUST ALSO COME GREAT RESPONSIBILITY. AND SO HE BECAME THE AMAZING
SPIDER-MAN
WORLD WAR G
FRED VAN LENTE WRITER
CORY HAMSCHER ARTIST
GURU eFX COLORISTS
DAVE SHARPE LETTERER
SCHERBERGER, HAMSCHER et GURU eFX COVER
DAVE SHARPE PRODUCTION
NATHAN COSBY ASSISTANT EDITOR
MARK PANICCIA EDITOR
JOE QUESADA EDITOR IN CHIEF
DAN BUCKLEY PUBLISHER

VISIT US AT
www.abdopublishing.com

Reinforced library bound edition published in 2008 by Spotlight, a division of the ABDO Publishing Group, 8000 West 78th Street, Edina, Minnesota 55439. Spotlight produces high-quality reinforced library bound editions for schools and libraries. Published by agreement with Marvel Characters, Inc.

Library of Congress Cataloging-in-Publication Data

Van Lente, Fred.
World War G / Fred Van Lente, writer ; Cory Hamscher, artist ; GURU eFX, colorists ; Dave Sharpe, letterer ; Scherberger, Hamscher et GURU eFX, cover. -- Reinforced library bound ed.
p. cm. -- (Spider-man)
"Marvel age"--Cover.
Revision of issue 22 of Marvel adventures Spider-man.
ISBN 978-1-59961-396-3
1. Graphic novels. I. Hamscher, Cory. II. Marvel adventures. Spider-man. 22. III. Title.

PN6728.S6V39 2008
741.5'973--dc22

2007020248

Spotlight

All Spotlight books have reinforced library bindings and are manufactured in the United States of America.

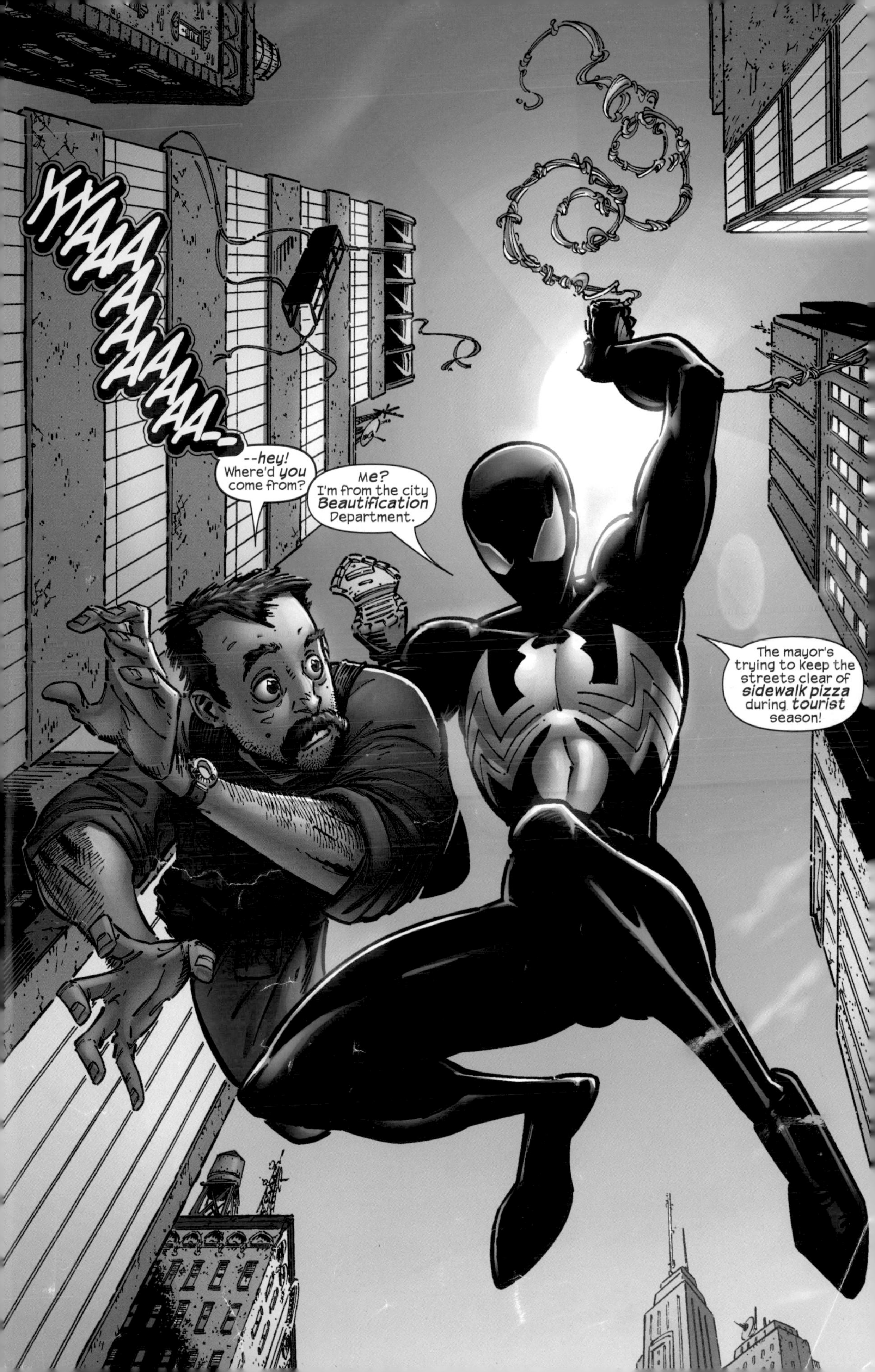
YYYAAAAAAAAAAA--
--hey! Where'd you come from?
Me? I'm from the city Beautification Department.
The mayor's trying to keep the streets clear of sidewalk pizza during tourist season!

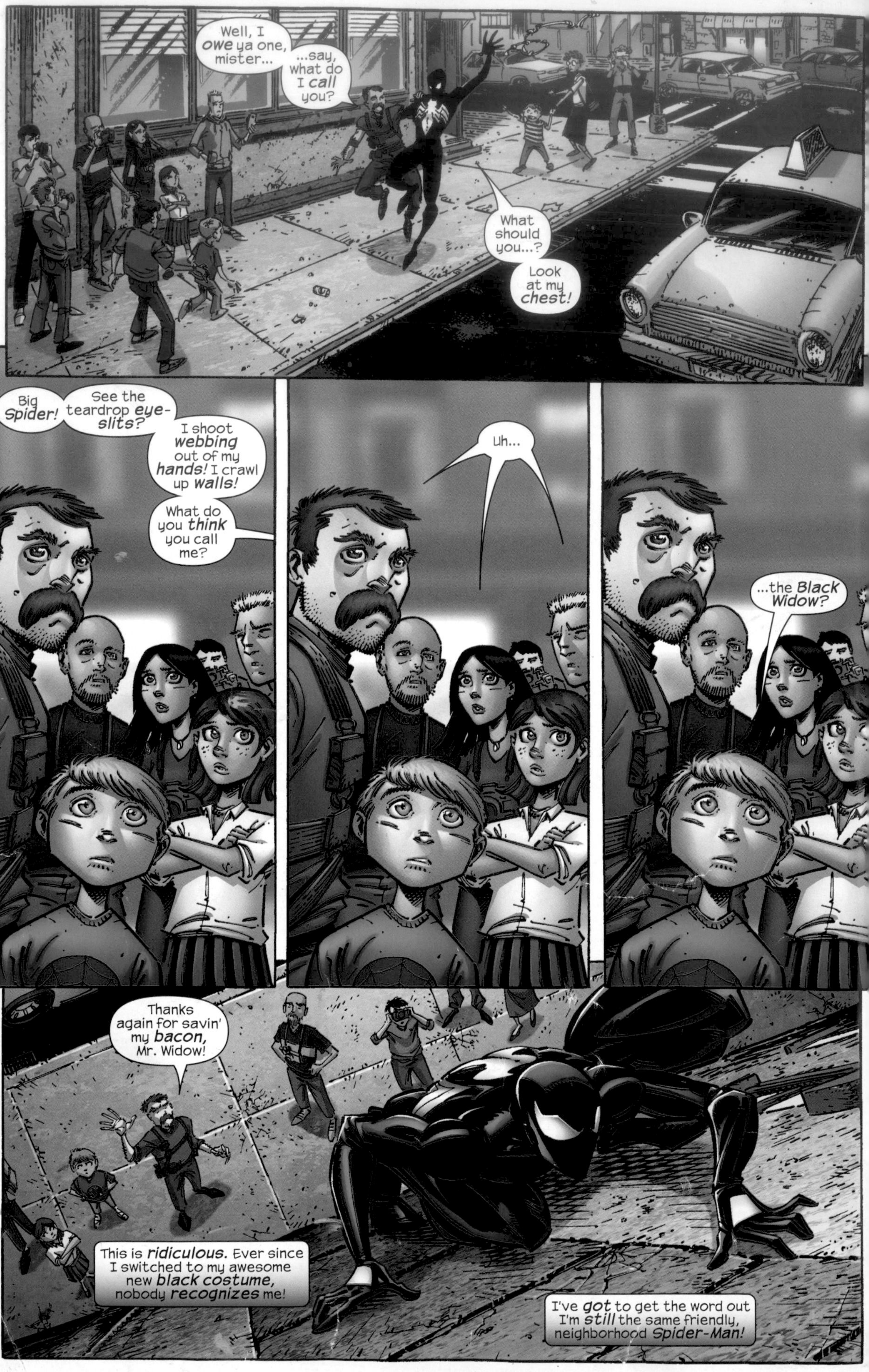
Well, I owe ya one, mister...
...say, what do I call you?
What should you...?
Look at my chest!
Big Spider!
See the teardrop eye-slits?
I shoot webbing out of my hands! I crawl up walls!
What do you think you call me?
Uh...
...the Black Widow?
Thanks again for savin' my bacon, Mr. Widow!
This is ridiculous. Ever since I switched to my awesome new black costume, nobody recognizes me!
I've got to get the word out I'm still the same friendly, neighborhood Spider-Man!

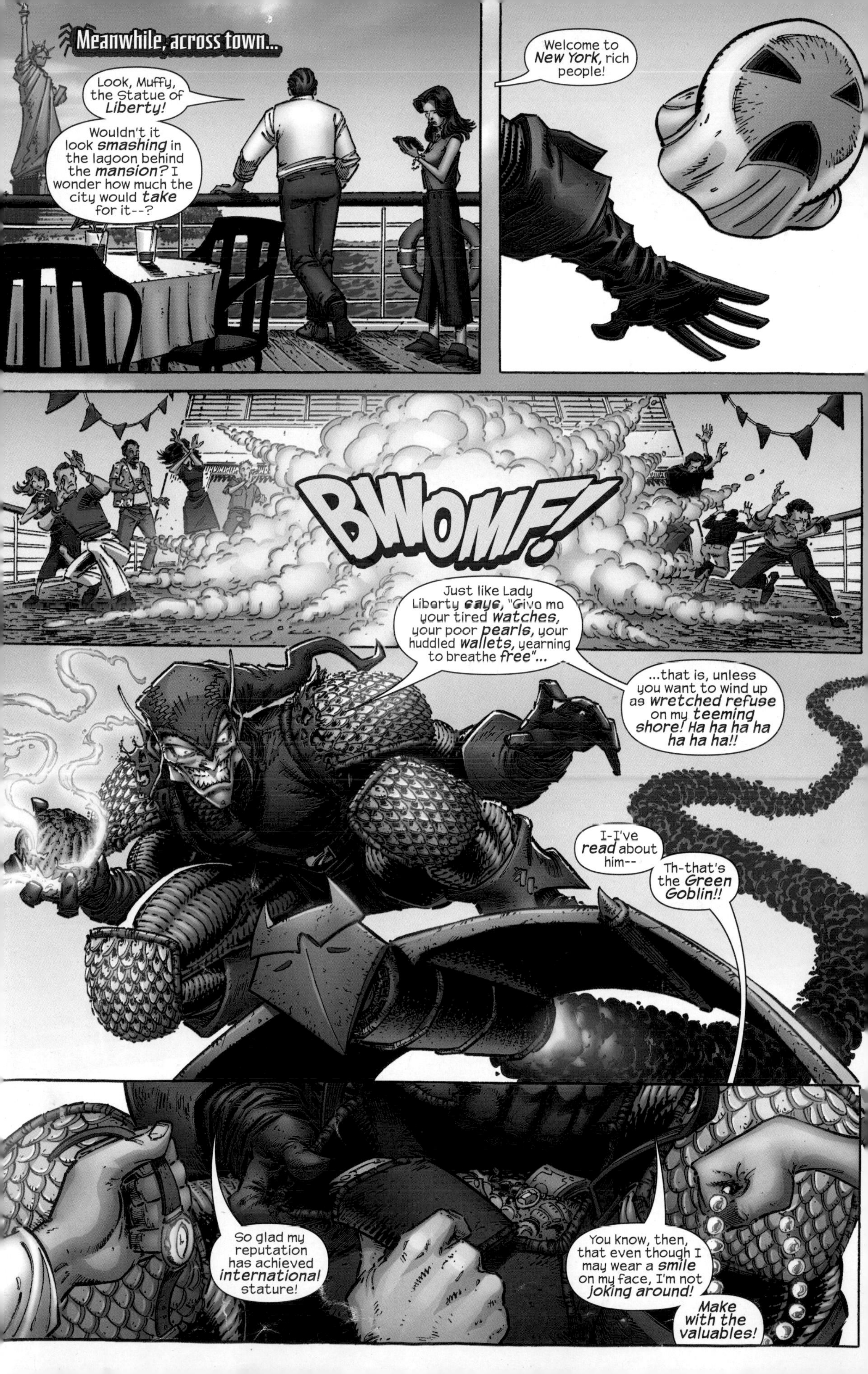

Meanwhile, across town...
Look, Muffy, the Statue of Liberty!
Wouldn't it look smashing in the lagoon behind the mansion? I wonder how much the city would take for it--?
Welcome to New York, rich people!
BWOMF!
Just like Lady Liberty says, "Give me your tired watches, your poor pearls, your huddled wallets, yearning to breathe free"...
...that is, unless you want to wind up as wretched refuse on my teeming shore! Ha ha ha ha ha ha ha!!
I-I've read about him--
Th-that's the Green Goblin!!
So glad my reputation has achieved international stature!
You know, then, that even though I may wear a smile on my face, I'm not joking around!
Make with the valuables!

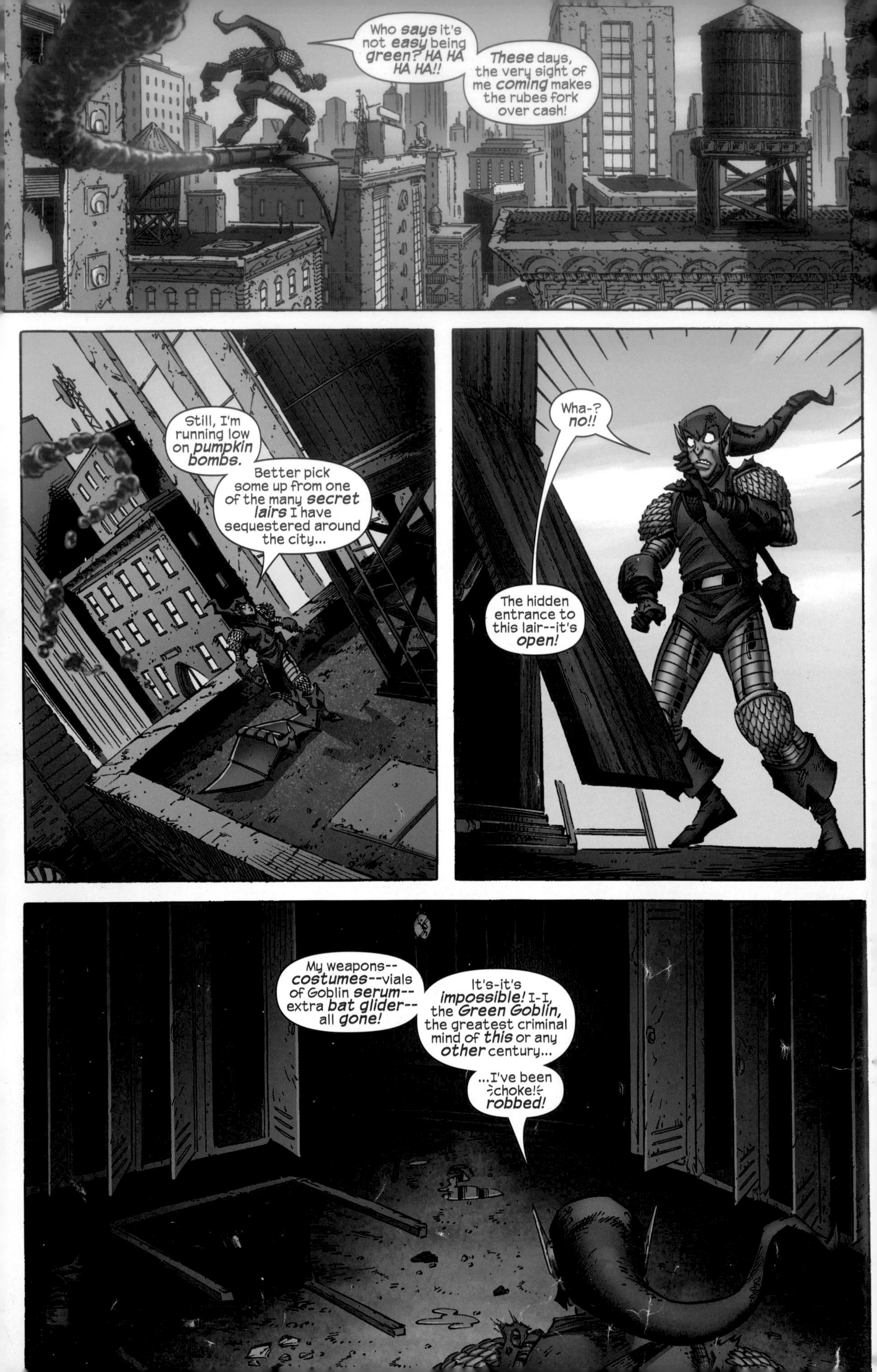
Who says it's not easy being green? HA HA HA HA!!
These days, the very sight of me coming makes the rubes fork over cash!
Still, I'm running low on pumpkin bombs.
Better pick some up from one of the many secret lairs I have sequestered around the city...
Wha-? no!!
The hidden entrance to this lair--it's open!
My weapons--costumes--vials of Goblin serum--extra bat glider--all gone!
It's-it's impossible! I-I, the Green Goblin, the greatest criminal mind of this or any other century...
...I've been *choke!* robbed!

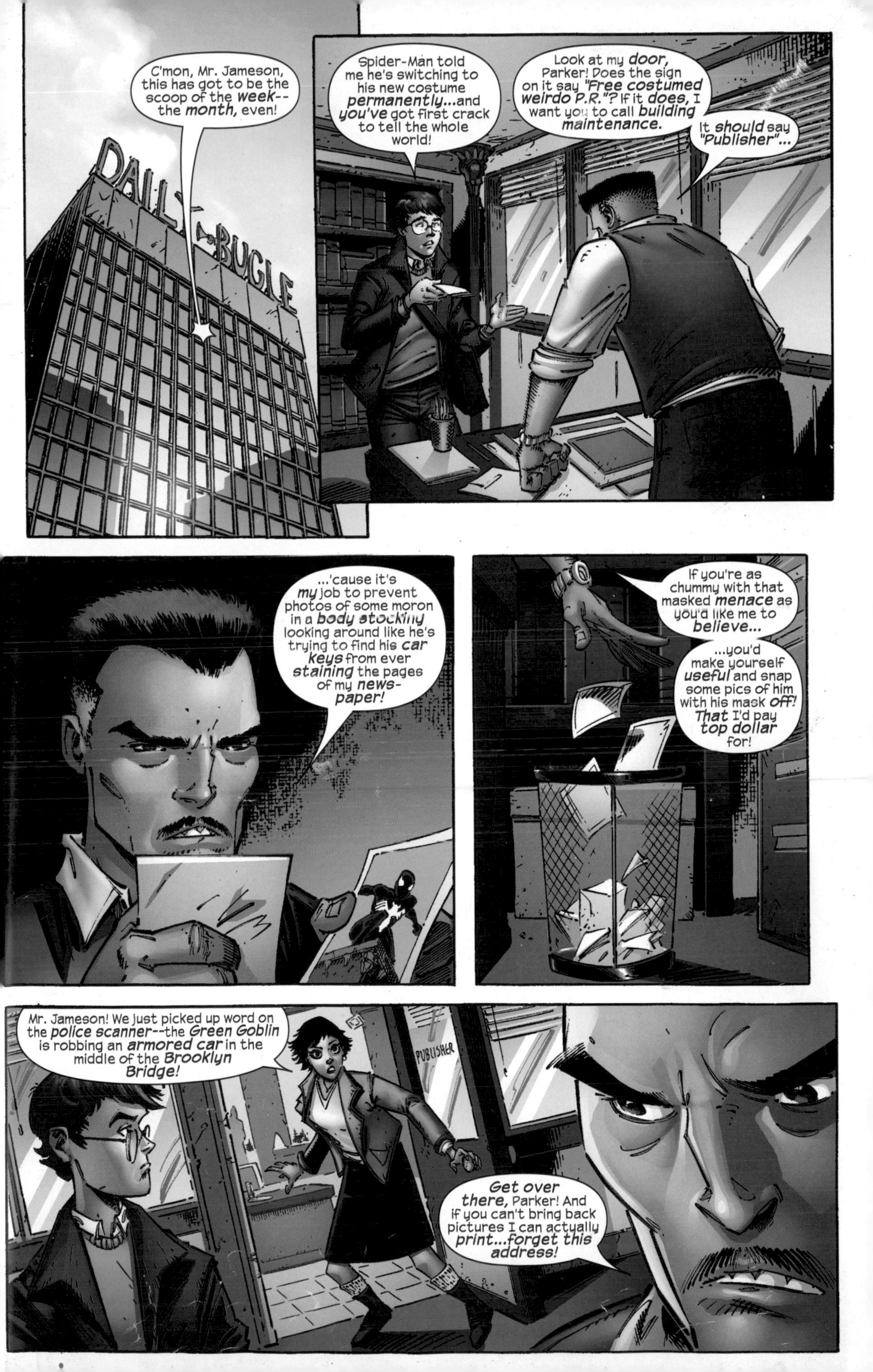
DAILY BUGLE
C'mon, Mr. Jameson, this has got to be the scoop of the week-- the month, even!
Spider-Man told me he's switching to his new costume permanently...and you've got first crack to tell the whole world!
Look at my door, Parker! Does the sign on it say "Free costumed weirdo P.R."? If it does, I want you to call building maintenance.
It should say "Publisher"...
...'cause it's my job to prevent photos of some moron in a body stocking looking around like he's trying to find his car keys from ever staining the pages of my news-paper!
If you're as chummy with that masked menace as you'd like me to believe...
...you'd make yourself useful and snap some pics of him with his mask off! That I'd pay top dollar for!
Mr. Jameson! We just picked up word on the police scanner--the Green Goblin is robbing an armored car in the middle of the Brooklyn Bridge!
PUBLISHER
Get over there, Parker! And if you can't bring back pictures I can actually print...forget this address!

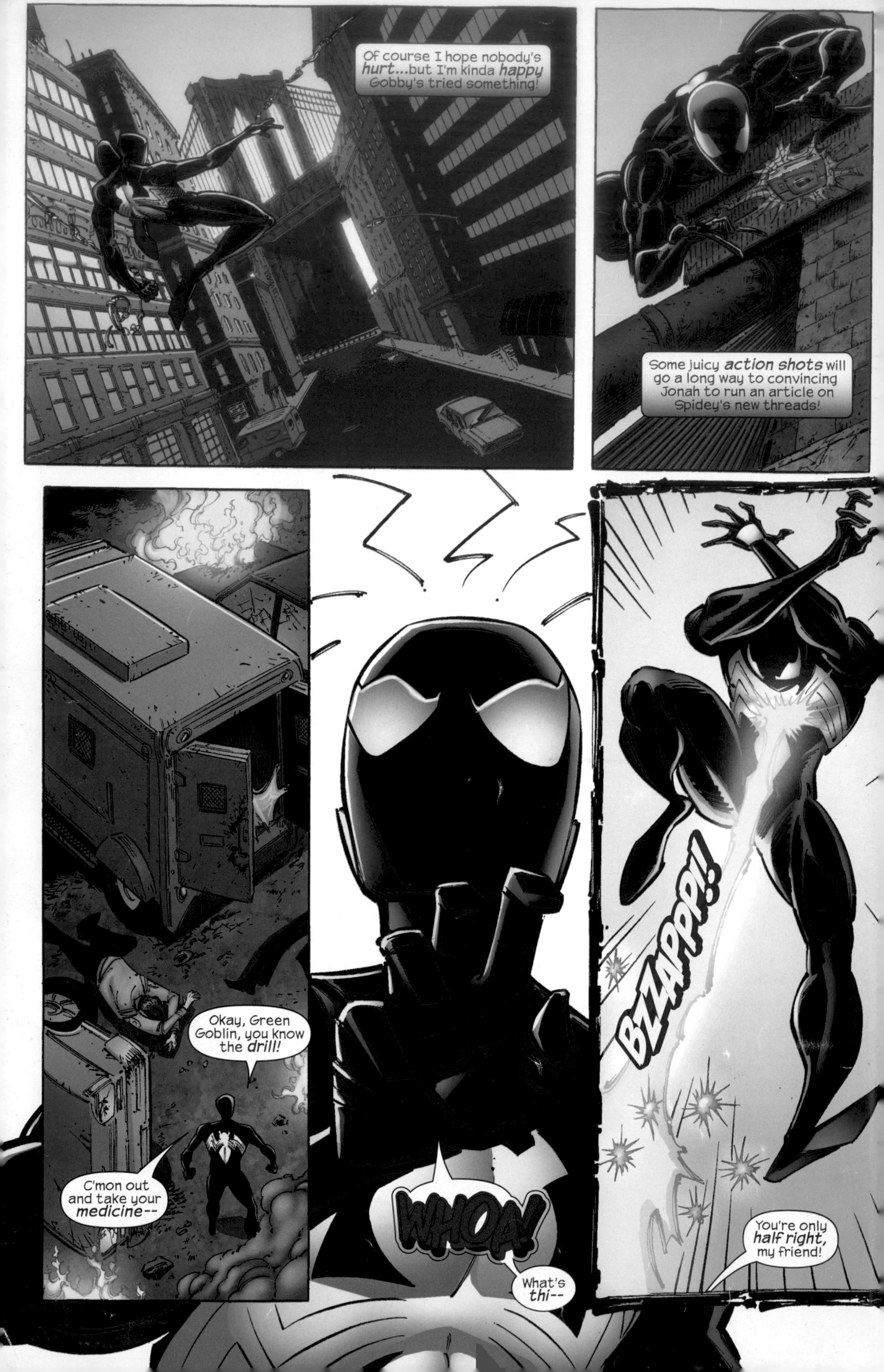
Of course I hope nobody's hurt...but I'm kinda happy Gobby's tried something!
Some juicy action shots will go a long way to convincing Jonah to run an article on Spidey's new threads!
Okay, Green Goblin, you know the drill!
C'mon out and take your medicine--
WHOA!
What's thi--
BZZAPP!!
You're only half right, my friend!

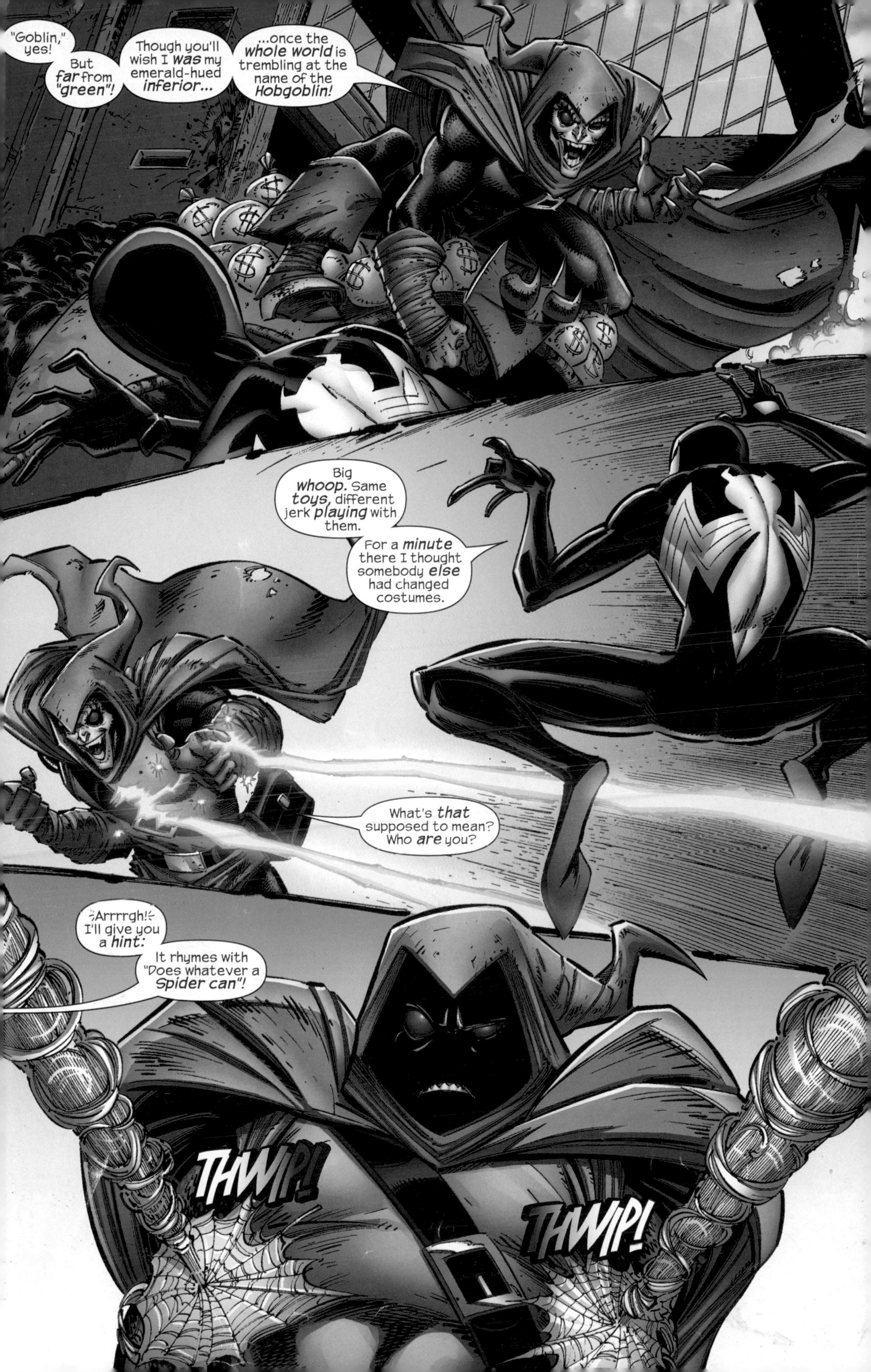
"Goblin," yes!
But far from "green"!
Though you'll wish I was my emerald-hued inferior...
...once the whole world is trembling at the name of the Hobgoblin!
Big whoop. Same toys, different jerk playing with them.
For a minute there I thought somebody else had changed costumes.
What's that supposed to mean? Who are you?
Arrrrgh! I'll give you a hint:
It rhymes with "Does whatever a Spider can"!
THWIP!
THWIP!

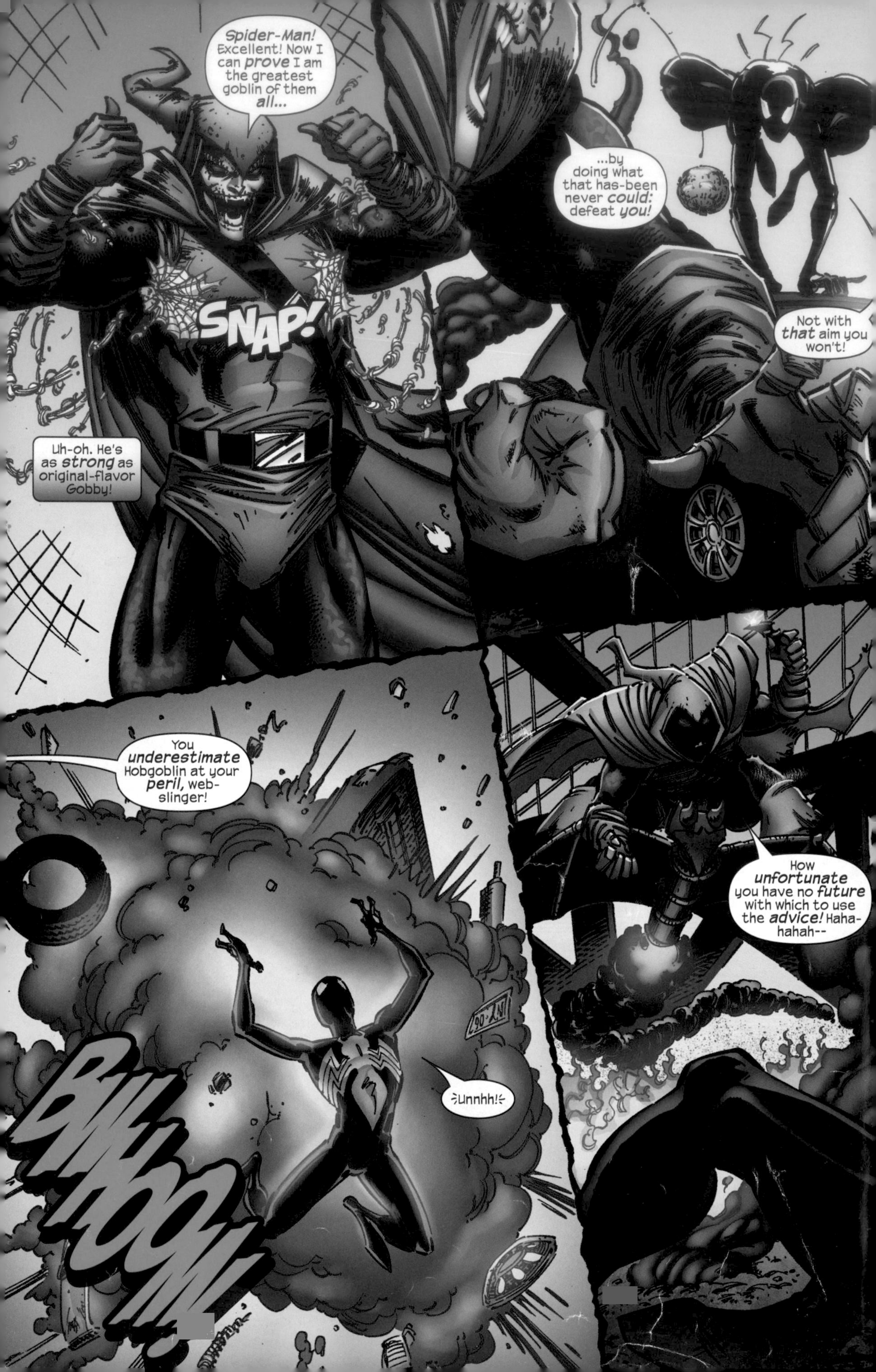
Spider-Man! Excellent! Now I can prove I am the greatest goblin of them all...
SNAP!
Uh-oh. He's as strong as original-flavor Gobby!
...by doing what that has-been never could: defeat you!
Not with that aim you won't!
You underestimate Hobgoblin at your peril, web-slinger!
Unnhh!
How unfortunate you have no future with which to use the advice! Haha-hahah--

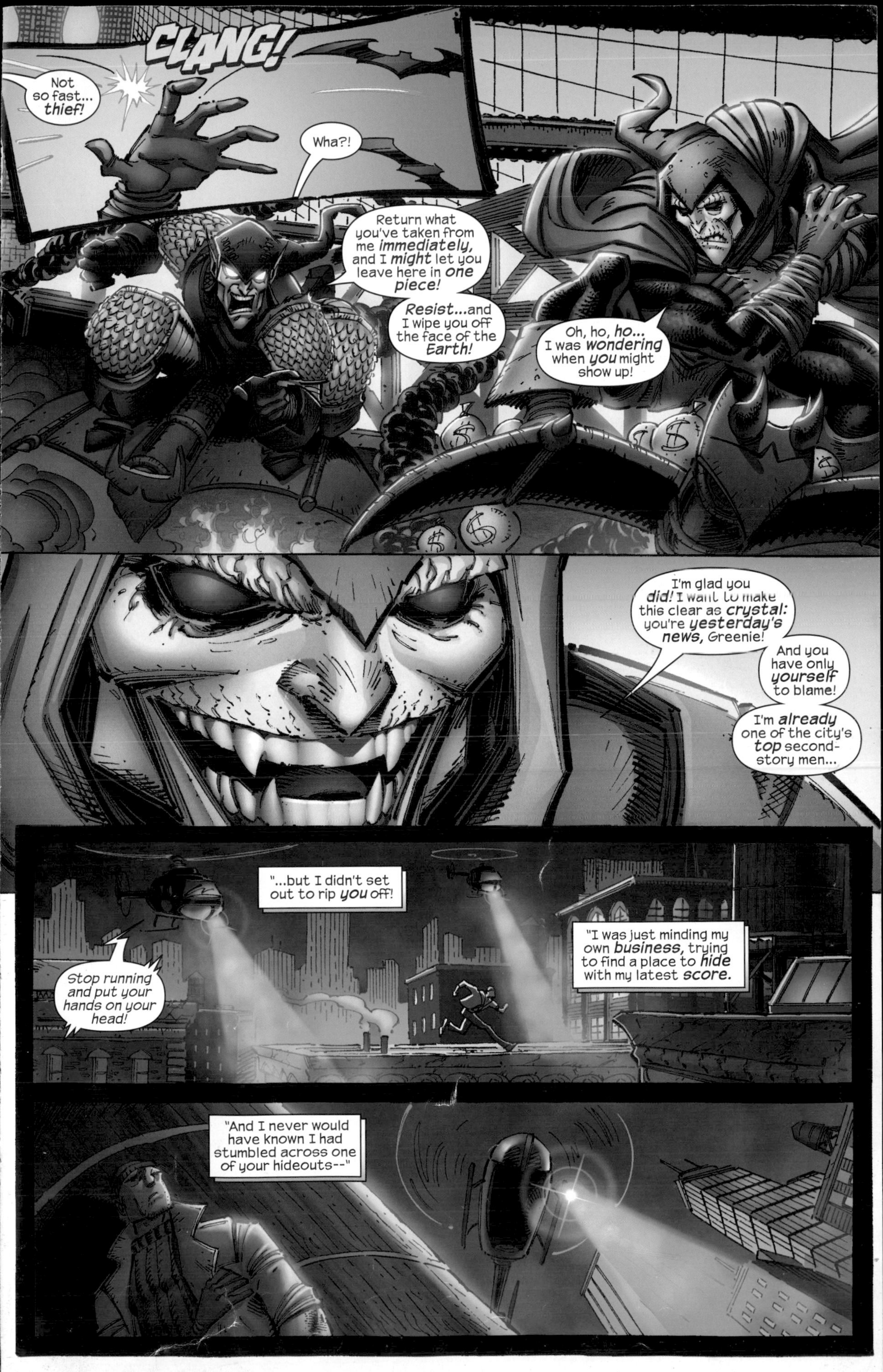
CLANG!
Not so fast... thief!
Wha?!
Return what you've taken from me immediately, and I might let you leave here in one piece!
Resist...and I wipe you off the face of the Earth!
Oh, ho, ho... I was wondering when you might show up!
I'm glad you did! I want to make this clear as crystal: you're yesterday's news, Greenie!
And you have only yourself to blame!
I'm already one of the city's top second-story men...
"...but I didn't set out to rip you off!
Stop running and put your hands on your head!
"I was just minding my own business, trying to find a place to hide with my latest score.
"And I never would have known I had stumbled across one of your hideouts--"

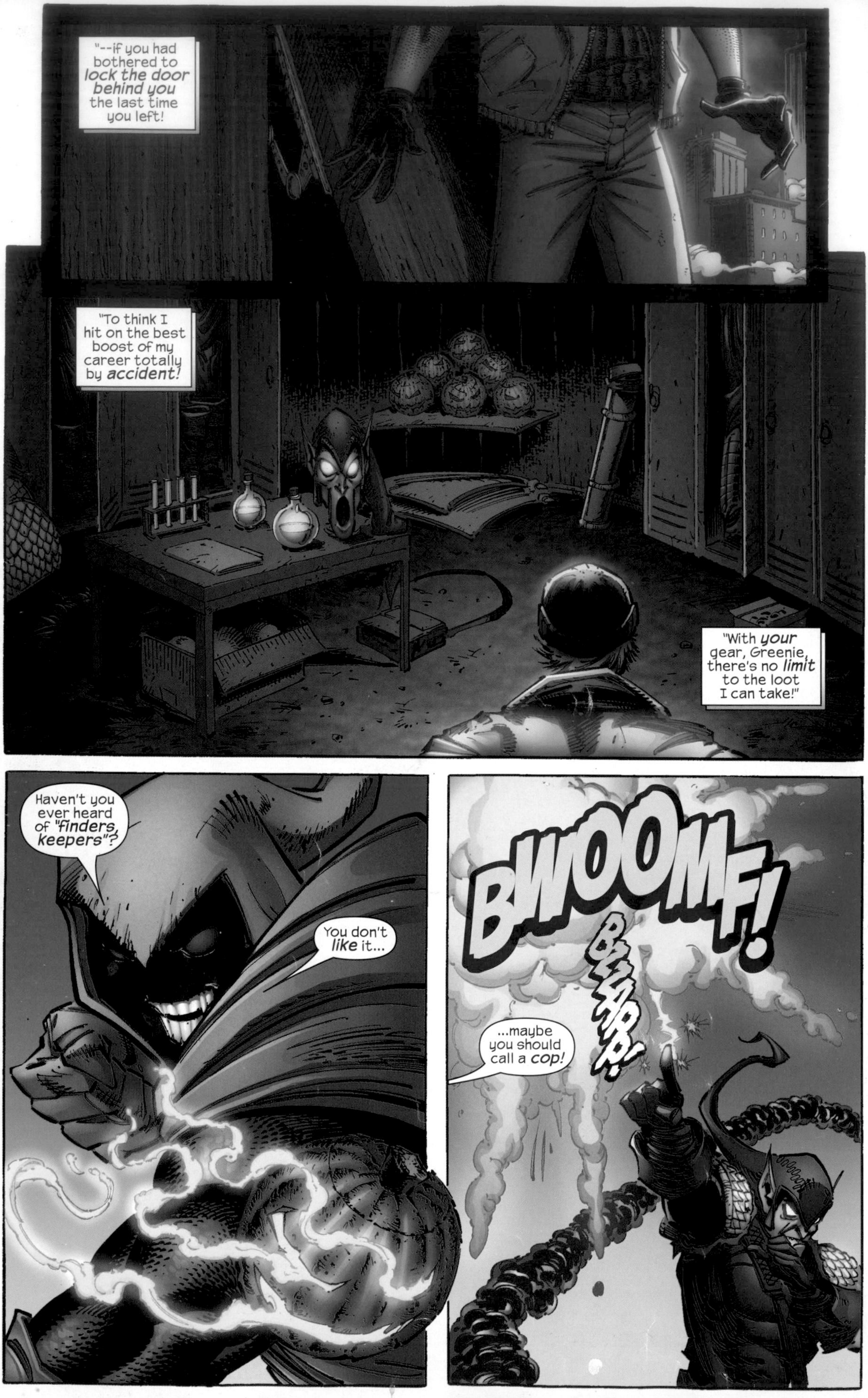
"--if you had bothered to lock the door behind you the last time you left!
"To think I hit on the best boost of my career totally by accident!
"With your gear, Greenie, there's no limit to the loot I can take!"
Haven't you ever heard of "finders, keepers"?
You don't like it...
BWOOMF!
BZZAPP!
...maybe you should call a cop!

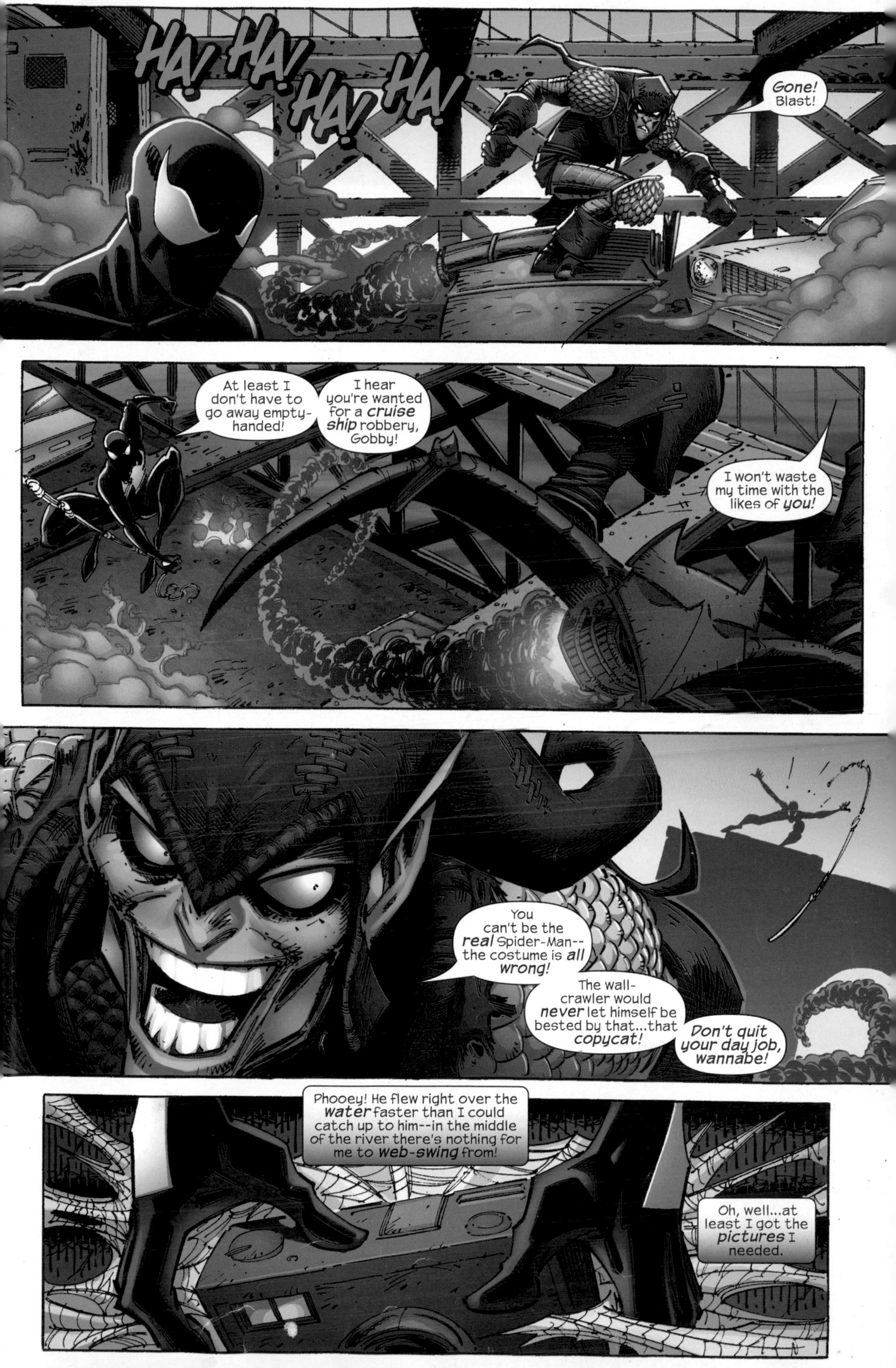
HA! HA! HA! HA!
Gone! Blast!
At least I don't have to go away empty-handed!
I hear you're wanted for a cruise ship robbery, Gobby!
I won't waste my time with the likes of you!
You can't be the real Spider-Man--the costume is all wrong!
The wall-crawler would never let himself be bested by that...that copycat!
Don't quit your day job, wannabe!
Phooey! He flew right over the water faster than I could catch up to him--in the middle of the river there's nothing for me to web-swing from!
Oh, well...at least I got the pictures I needed.

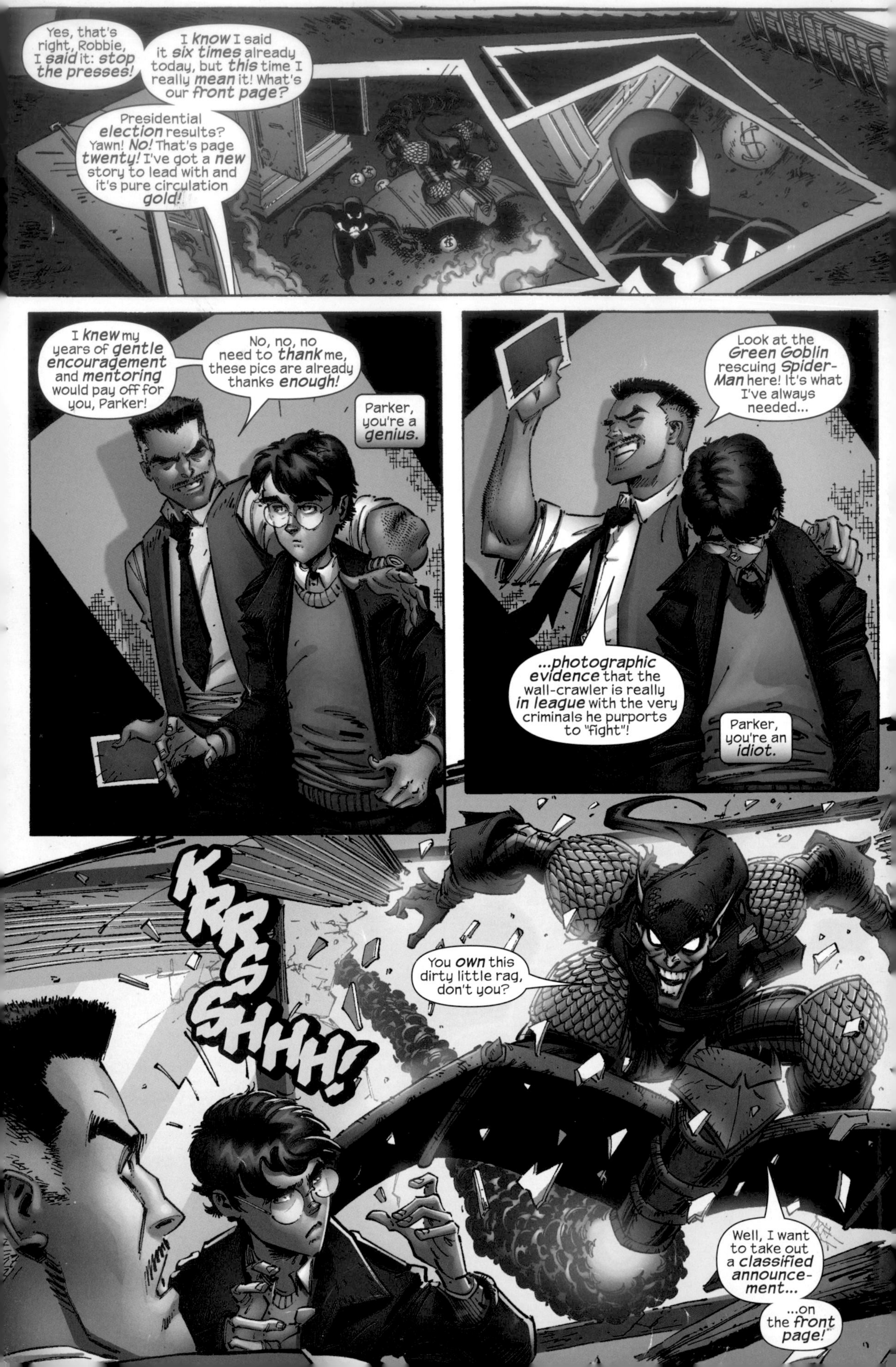

Yes, that's right, Robbie, I said it: stop the presses!
I know I said it six times already today, but this time I really mean it! What's our front page?
Presidential election results? Yawn! No! That's page twenty! I've got a new story to lead with and it's pure circulation gold!
I knew my years of gentle encouragement and mentoring would pay off for you, Parker!
No, no, no need to thank me, these pics are already thanks enough!
Parker, you're a genius.
Look at the Green Goblin rescuing Spider-Man here! It's what I've always needed...
...photographic evidence that the wall-crawler is really in league with the very criminals he purports to "fight"!
Parker, you're an idiot.
KRRSSHHH!
You own this dirty little rag, don't you?
Well, I want to take out a classified announce-ment...
...on the front page!

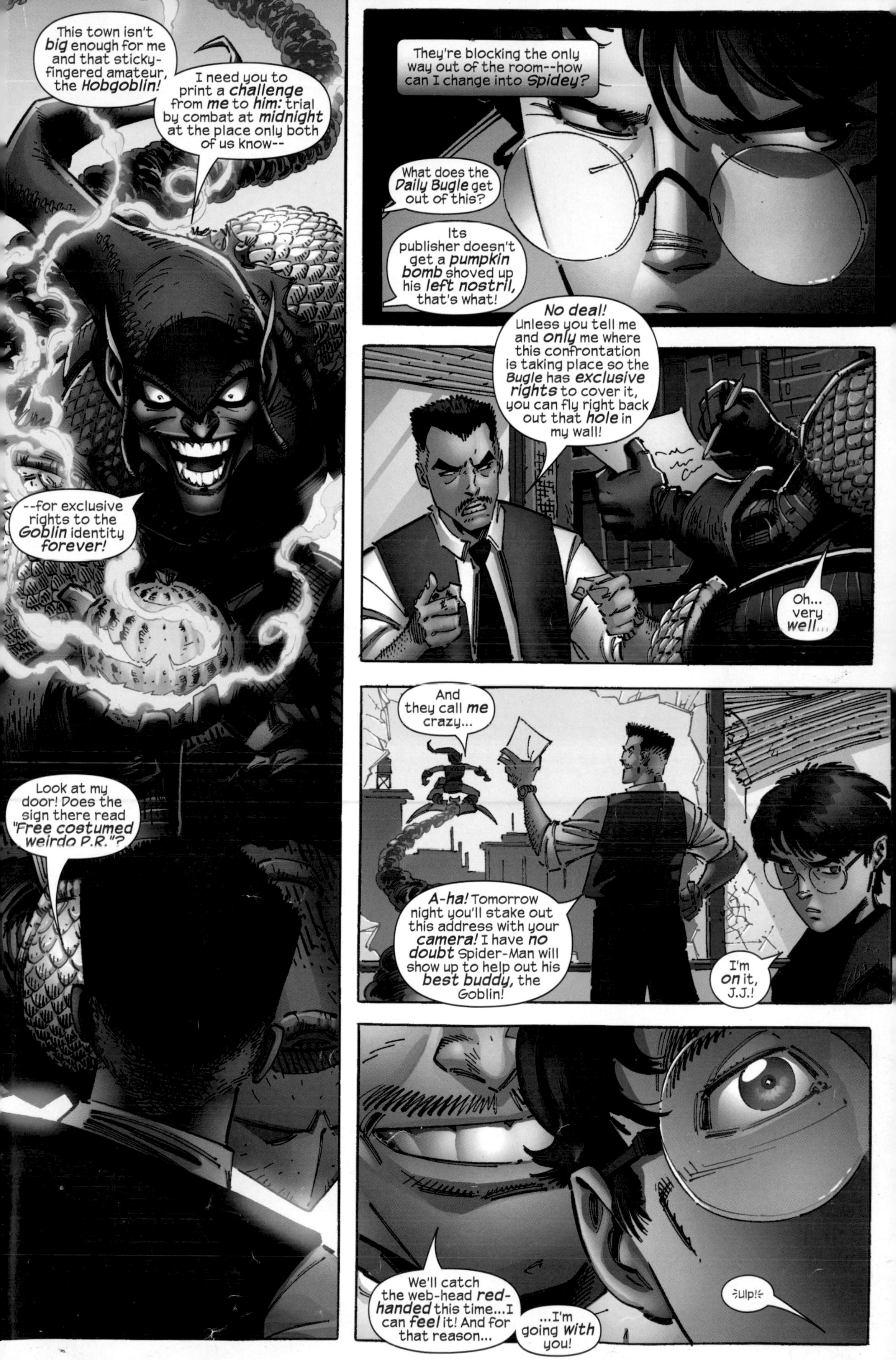
This town isn't big enough for me and that sticky-fingered amateur, the Hobgoblin!
I need you to print a challenge from me to him: trial by combat at midnight at the place only both of us know--
--for exclusive rights to the Goblin identity forever!
Look at my door! Does the sign there read "Free costumed weirdo P.R."?
They're blocking the only way out of the room--how can I change into Spidey?
What does the Daily Bugle get out of this?
Its publisher doesn't get a pumpkin bomb shoved up his left nostril, that's what!
No deal! Unless you tell me and only me where this confrontation is taking place so the Bugle has exclusive rights to cover it, you can fly right back out that hole in my wall!
Oh... very well...
And they call me crazy...
A-ha! Tomorrow night you'll stake out this address with your camera! I have no doubt Spider-Man will show up to help out his best buddy, the Goblin!
I'm on it, J.J.!
We'll catch the web-head red-handed this time...I can feel it! And for that reason...
...I'm going with you!
Ulp!

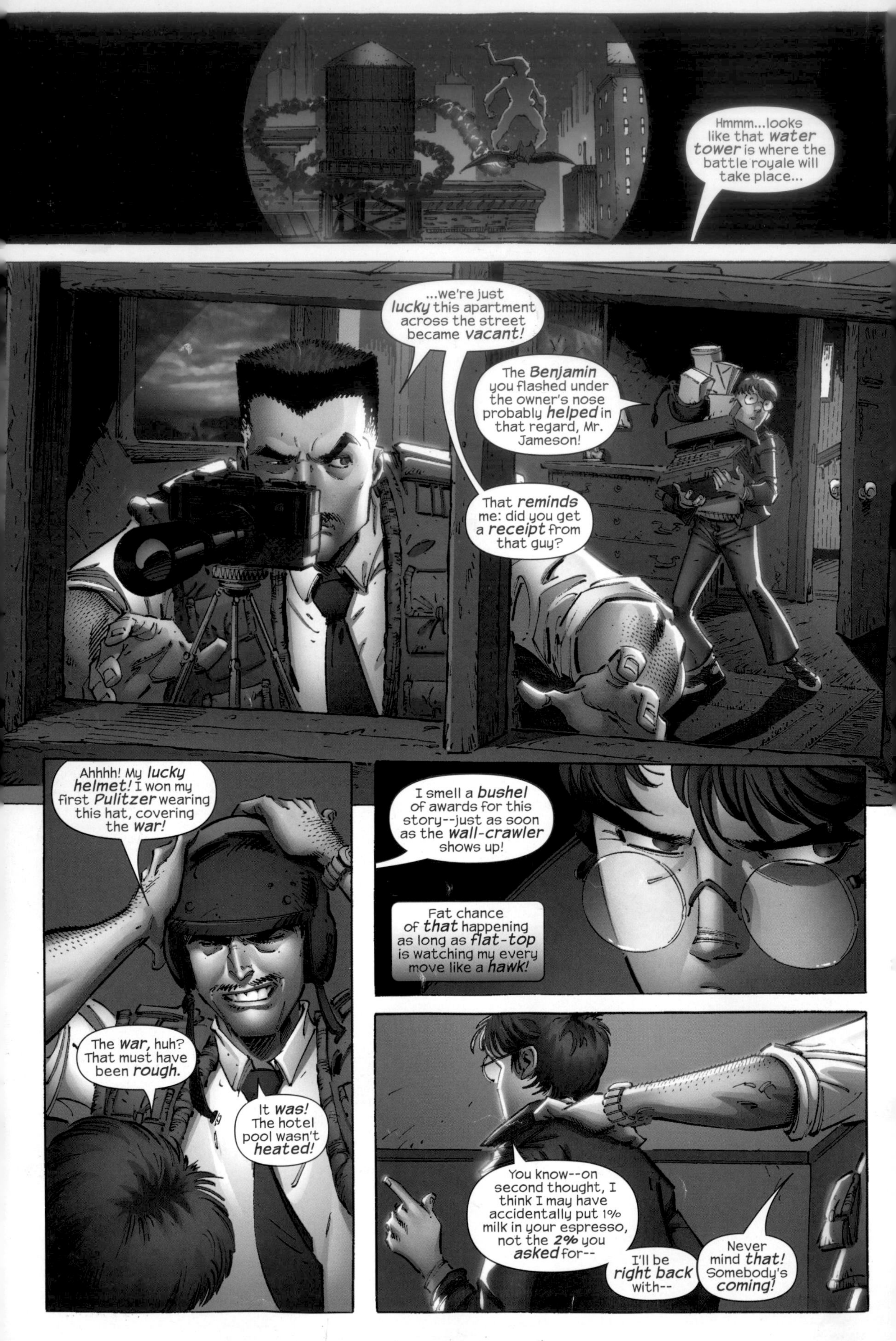
Hmmm...looks like that water tower is where the battle royale will take place...
...we're just lucky this apartment across the street became vacant!
The Benjamin you flashed under the owner's nose probably helped in that regard, Mr. Jameson!
That reminds me: did you get a receipt from that guy?
Ahhhh! My lucky helmet! I won my first Pulitzer wearing this hat, covering the war!
The war, huh? That must have been rough.
It was! The hotel pool wasn't heated!
I smell a bushel of awards for this story--just as soon as the wall-crawler shows up!
Fat chance of that happening as long as flat-top is watching my every move like a hawk!
You know--on second thought, I think I may have accidentally put 1% milk in your espresso, not the 2% you asked for--
I'll be right back with--
Never mind that! Somebody's coming!

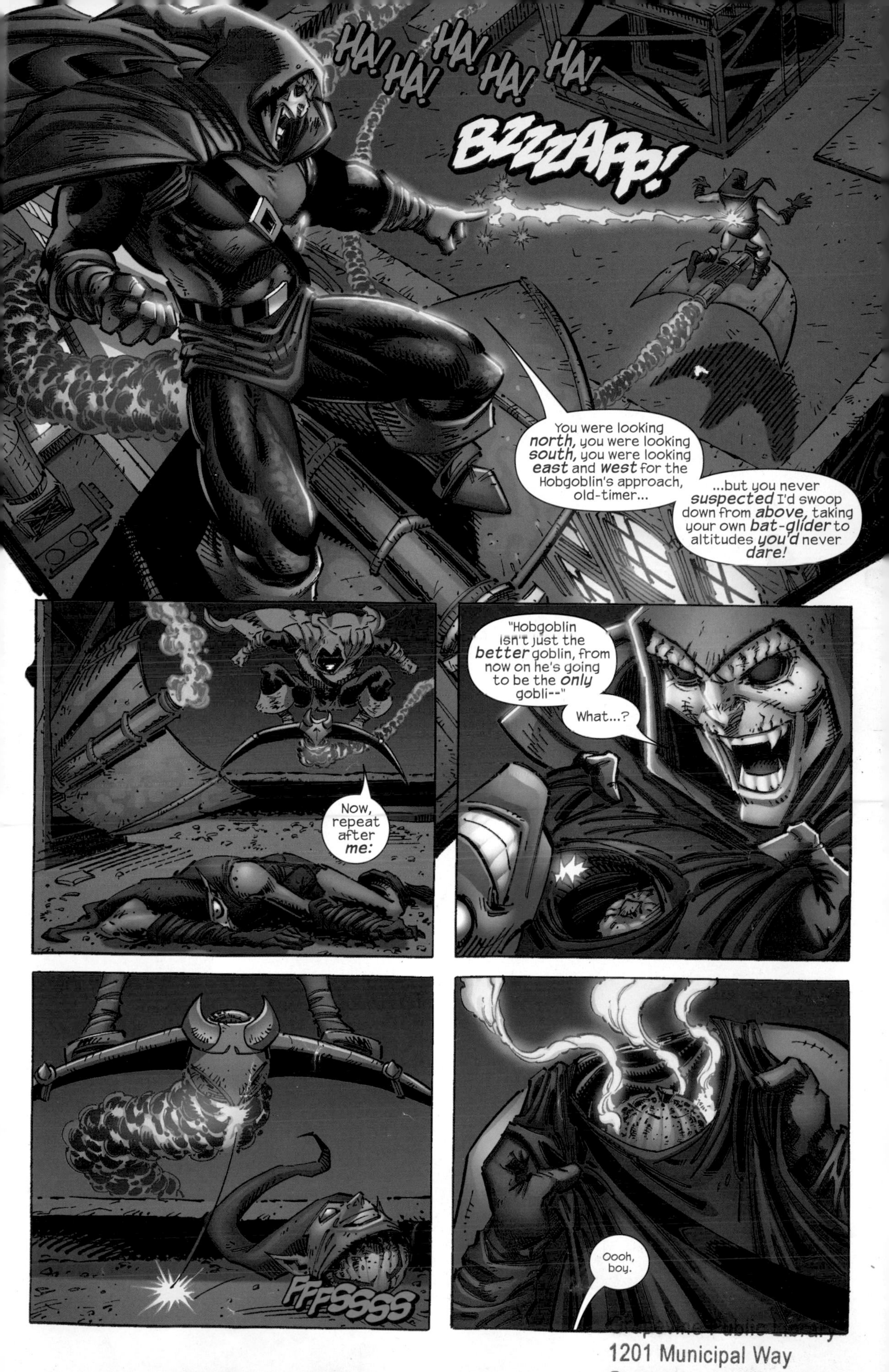
HA! HA! HA! HA! HA!
BZZZAPP!
You were looking north, you were looking south, you were looking east and west for the Hobgoblin's approach, old-timer...
...but you never suspected I'd swoop down from above, taking your own bat-glider to altitudes you'd never dare!
Now, repeat after me:
"Hobgoblin isn't just the better goblin, from now on he's going to be the only gobli--"
What...?
FFFSSSS
Oooh, boy.

BWHOOM!
AHAHAHAHAHA!
Didn't anyone ever tell you to always bet on experience, thief?
Wait-- no--
Blast! I can't see if Spider-Man has arrived through all those flames!
Somebody's going to get hurt if I don't stop these idiots!
I'm gonna have to give up my secret identity in a minute--
INCOMING!
Wait! Unless--
--the ghosts are smoke bombs, if I remember correctly...

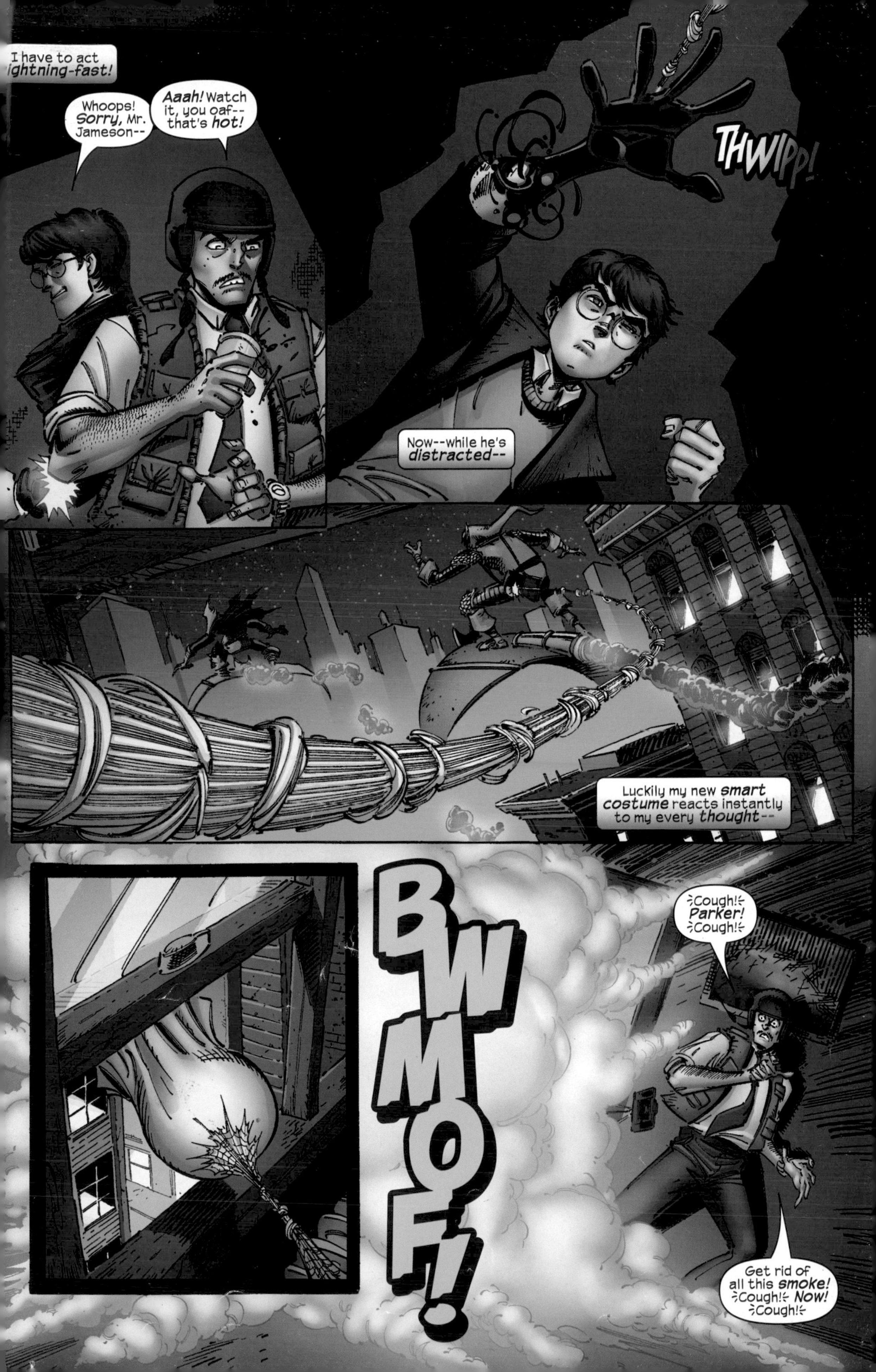
I have to act lightning-fast!
Whoops! Sorry, Mr. Jameson--
Aaah! Watch it, you oaf-- that's hot!
THWIPP!
Now--while he's distracted--
Luckily my new smart costume reacts instantly to my every thought--
BWMOF!
Cough! Parker! Cough!
Get rid of all this smoke! Cough! Now! Cough!

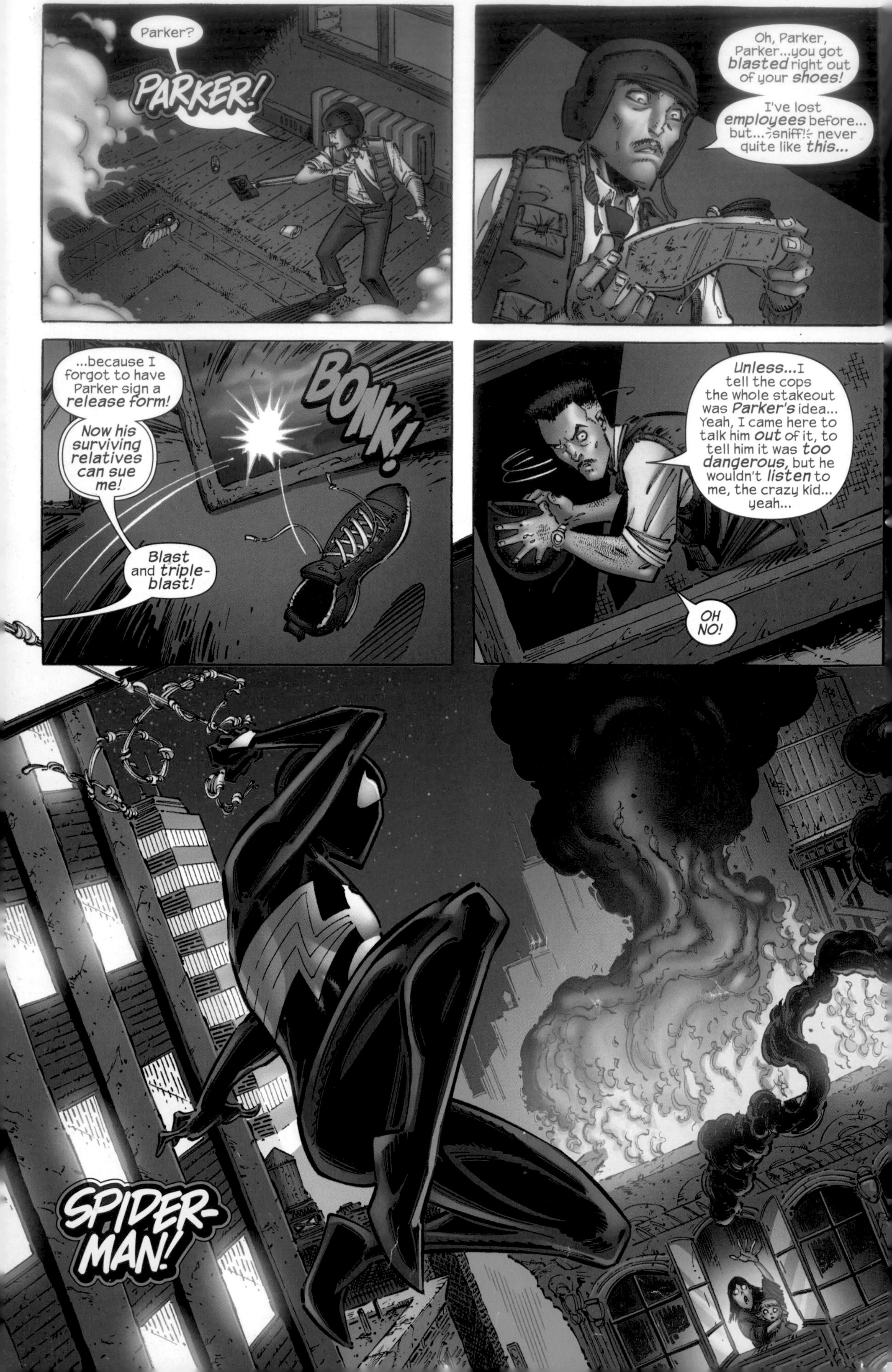
Parker?
PARKER!
Oh, Parker, Parker...you got blasted right out of your shoes!
I've lost employees before... but... sniff! never quite like this...
...because I forgot to have Parker sign a release form!
Now his surviving relatives can sue me!
Blast and triple-blast!
BONK!
Unless...I tell the cops the whole stakeout was Parker's idea... Yeah, I came here to talk him out of it, to tell him it was too dangerous, but he wouldn't listen to me, the crazy kid... yeah...
OH NO!
SPIDER-MAN!

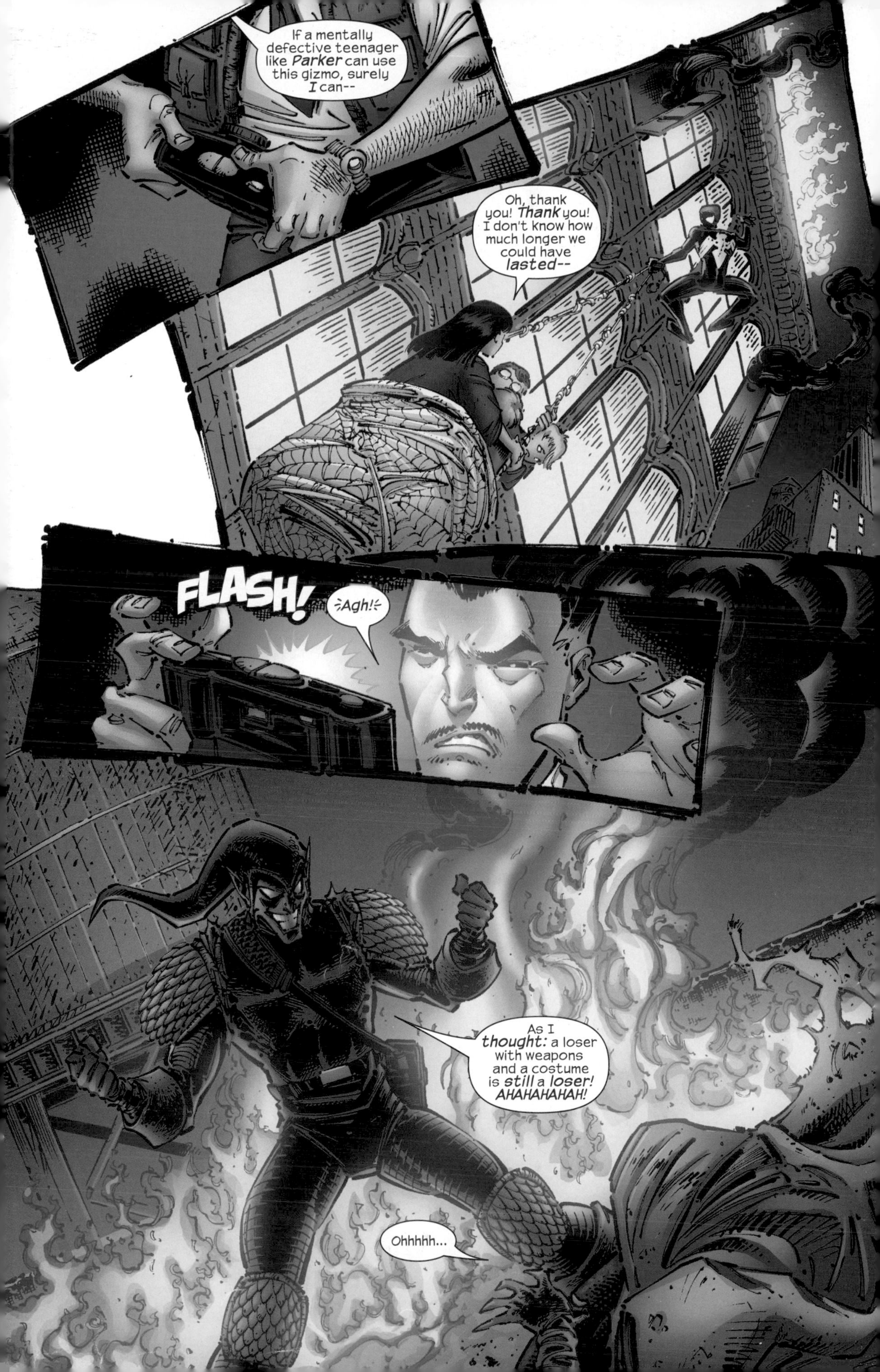
If a mentally defective teenager like Parker can use this gizmo, surely I can--
Oh, thank you! Thank you! I don't know how much longer we could have lasted--
FLASH!
Agh!
As I thought: a loser with weapons and a costume is still a loser! AHAHAHAHAH!
Ohhhhh...

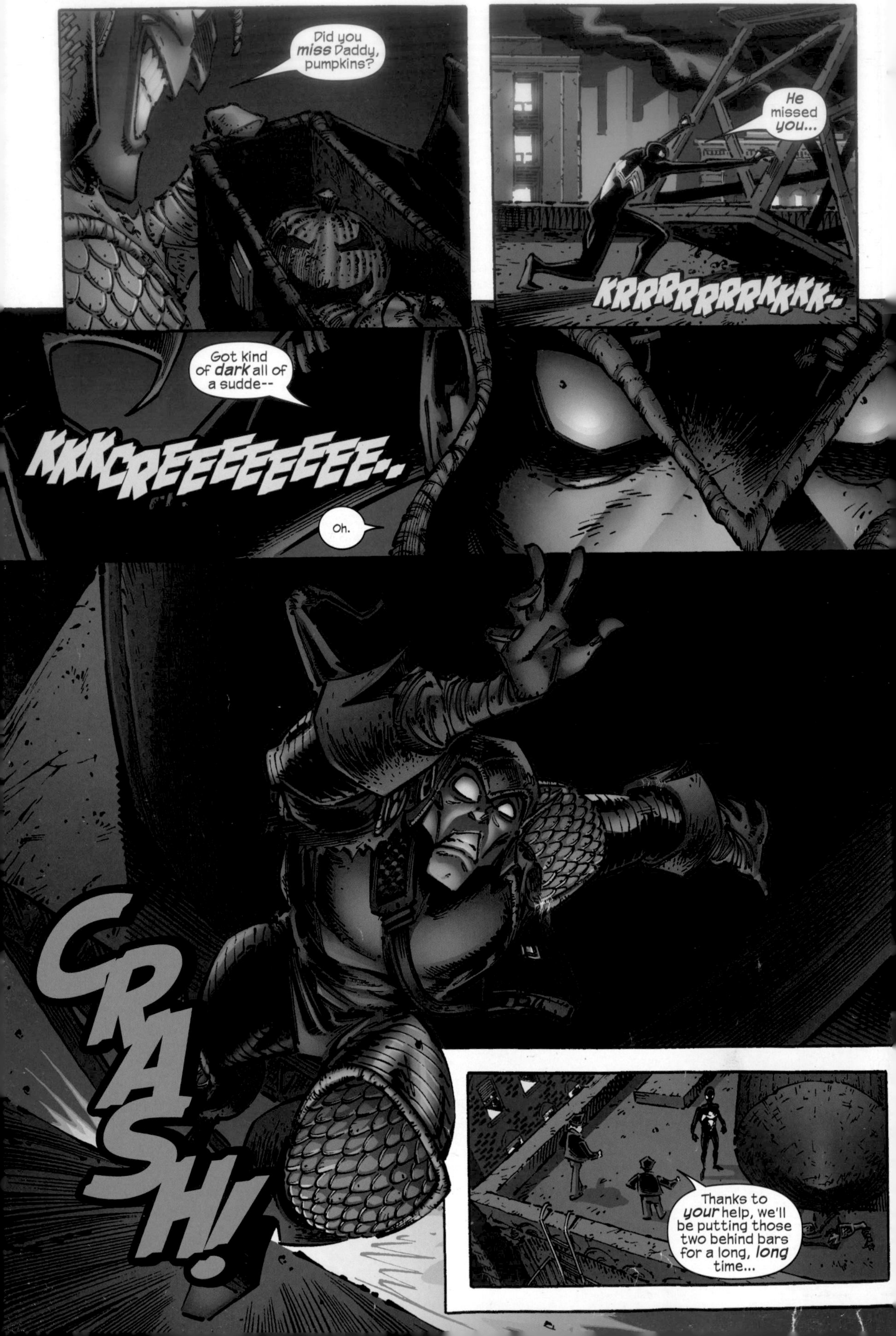
Did you *miss* Daddy, pumpkins?
He missed *you*...
KRRRRRRRKKKK..
Got kind of *dark* all of a sudde--
KKKCREEEEEEEEEE..
Oh.
CRASH!
Thanks to *your* help, we'll be putting those two behind bars for a long, *long* time...

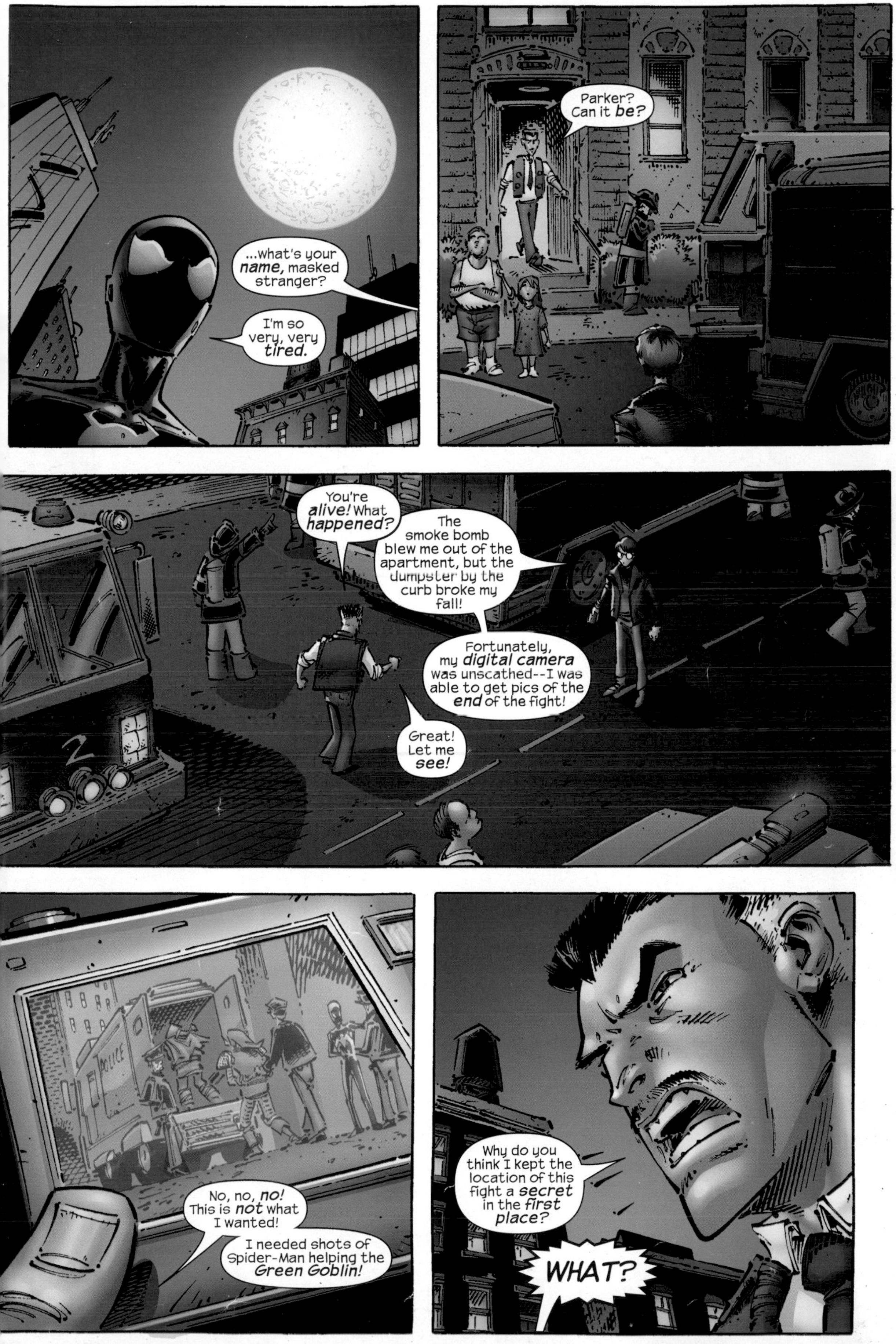
...what's your name, masked stranger?
I'm so very, very tired.
Parker? Can it be?
You're alive! What happened?
The smoke bomb blew me out of the apartment, but the dumpster by the curb broke my fall!
Fortunately, my digital camera was unscathed--I was able to get pics of the end of the fight!
Great! Let me see!
POLICE
No, no, no! This is not what I wanted!
I needed shots of Spider-Man helping the Green Goblin!
Why do you think I kept the location of this fight a secret in the first place?
WHAT?

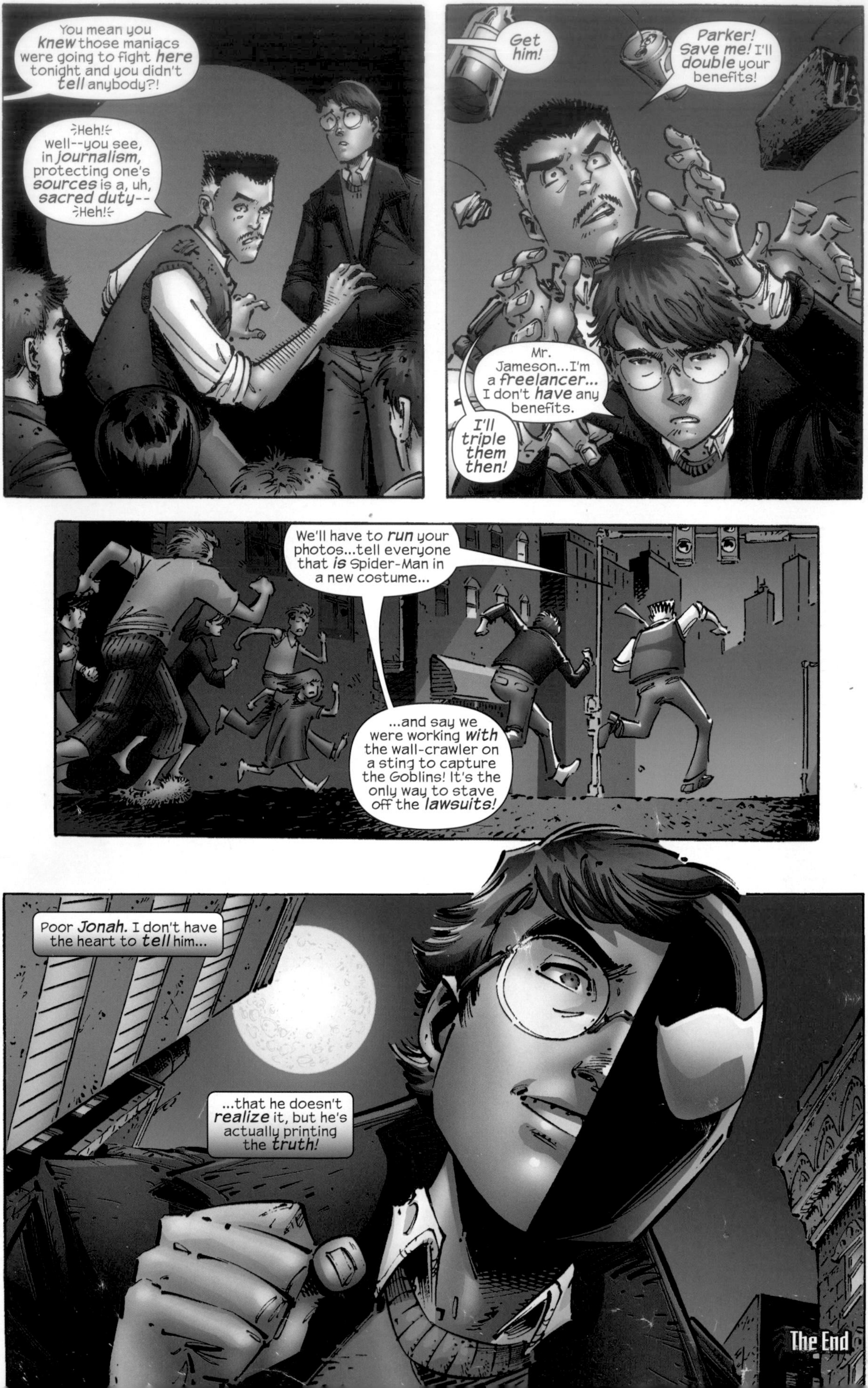
You mean you knew those maniacs were going to fight here tonight and you didn't tell anybody?!
Heh! well--you see, in journalism, protecting one's sources is a, uh, sacred duty-- Heh!
Get him!
Parker! Save me! I'll double your benefits!
Mr. Jameson...I'm a freelancer... I don't have any benefits.
I'll triple them then!
We'll have to run your photos...tell everyone that is Spider-Man in a new costume...
...and say we were working with the wall-crawler on a sting to capture the Goblins! It's the only way to stave off the lawsuits!
Poor Jonah. I don't have the heart to tell him...
...that he doesn't realize it, but he's actually printing the truth!
The End